Oh no!

Story by Eliza Comodromos
Illustrations by Mark Weber

Dr. Judith Nadell, Series Editor

"What do you have?" said Victor.

"I have a ham sandwich," said Robert.

"What do **you** have?" said Robert.

"I have chicken," said Victor.

"What more do you have?" said Victor.

"Oh no, a banana," said Robert.

"What more do **you** have?" said Robert.

"Oh no, an apple," said Victor.

"Do you like apples?" said Victor.

"Yes, I like apples!" said Robert.

"Do you like bananas?" said Robert.

"Yes, I like bananas!" said Victor.

"Let's swap!" said Victor.

"Yum, yum!"